Mister B

By Elizabeth Stevens

Illustrated by Daniela Frongia

ISBN13: 978-1484018644
ISBN10: 1484018648

Copyright © 2012 Elizabeth Stevens

This book is dedicated to my daughter, Jennifer, for being the inspiration for the story, and to my husband, James, who said to me, "You should write it as a children's book."

ONCE UPON A TIME there was a little girl named
Julie. She was so excited because she was going to take
a very big test at her karate school. If she passed the test,
she would get her black belt.

She practiced and practiced and practiced.

But Julie had a problem.
She got scared and nervous whenever
she tried to do her flying side kick in front
of people, or even animal friends.

No matter how hard she
tried, Julie couldn't do her best
in front of anyone. Julie didn't
know what was wrong.

Julie's Aunt Mary came to visit on the day
of the big black belt test.
Aunt Mary was Julie's favorite aunt.
It seemed like Aunt Mary knew everything.

That afternoon, while Julie's parents were getting ready to go to the test, Aunt Mary said, "Julie, why don't you practice one more time before we go?" Julie said, "Okay."
She put on her karate uniform and began to practice in front of Aunt Mary.

Julie did well until she started to do her flying side kick.
One time she couldn't jump high enough. The next time
she forgot which foot she was supposed to kick with.
Julie started crying. Aunt Mary gave her a big hug
and asked, "Why are you crying?"
Julie said, "Because I can do the flying
side kick when I'm all by myself, but
not when anyone is watching me."

Aunt Mary whispered to Julie,
"I have a secret to share with you."
Julie got excited because she loved
secrets.
"It's a special kind of secret,"
whispered Aunt Mary. "One that
you can tell all your friends."

"It's about Mister D," Aunt Mary said.
"What does the D stand for?" Julie asked.
"The D stands for doubt," said Aunt Mary.

I'm never going to get it right

I can't do it

I'm scared

"What does he do?" asked Julie.
"He tries to make it so you can't do
your best," said Aunt Mary, "He's not your friend."
Julie said, "I can't see him, though. Where is he?"
Aunt Mary said, "He's very hard to see, but you know
he's there when you say things like:
'I can't do it.'
'I'm never going to get it right.'
'I'm scared.' "

Julie asked, "How can I make Mister D go away?"
Aunt Mary told her that the only way to make
Mister D go away was to ignore him, no matter
how hard he tried to bother you.

"What if I can't ignore him?" asked Julie.

"Oh, Dear," said
Aunt Mary,
"Mister D is
making you
doubt yourself."

It was time for the big black belt test. Julie and the other students were lined up in front of the karate teacher. The teacher said loudly, "Okay, students, do we practice karate on our mom, or dad, or sister, or brother?" The students yelled out, "No, Sir!" "Do we practice karate on our cat, or on our dog?" The students yelled again, "No, Sir!" The teacher smiled and said, "Good, and also not on strangers, friends, or your furniture." The students all giggled.

The testing started.
Aunt Mary and Julie sat next to each other. They watched the other students test for their black belts. Aunt Mary told Julie that she saw Mister D everywhere. "I hope that everyone can ignore him," said Julie. She was hoping that she could ignore him, too.

Then it was Julie's turn to test. She stepped
onto the mat in front of everyone.
Aunt Mary looked all over for Mister D.
She couldn't find him anywhere.

Julie was doing great. She even had
a big smile on her face.
The hardest part was coming up.

It was time for Julie to do her flying side kick.
Just as Julie started to jump, Aunt Mary saw
Mister D sneak out behind her.

Aunt Mary yelled, "Julie!"
Julie jumped high in the air
and did her side kick at the
same time.
Julie shouted, "Go away,
Mister D!"

Mister D ran away and Julie landed perfectly.
Julie passed the test. She earned her black belt!
Everyone just clapped and clapped.
Aunt Mary and Julie's parents were very proud of her.

The next day, Julie looked out the window and saw her friend Daniel fall off his new bike.
He said, "Oh, I'm never going to learn how to ride!"

Julie ran out of the house.
"Mister D, you leave my friend
Daniel alone!" she shouted.
"Who's Mister D?"
asked Daniel.
"Come here,"
said Julie,
"and I'll tell you
a very special secret."

THE END

Photo by Robert Daggs

Author:
Elizabeth Stevens is a Boston-born screen and television writer-producer. She lives in South Pasadena, California with her husband and frequent collaborator, James Bruner, and their family. For more information, go to MisterDbook.com and BrunerandStevens.com.

Illustrator:
Daniela Frongia was born in Cagliari, Italy and currently lives in London, UK. She has dedicated herself to illustrating children's books and works with authors and publishers from all around the world. For more information, go to caisairbrush.com.

Made in the USA
Monee, IL
09 June 2020